Abba, my Father

Poetry of faith written from the heart

QUINN GRAW

Quinn Graw

Wholesale discounts for book orders are available
through Ingram or Spring Arbor Distributors.

ISBN

978-1-77302-020-4 (paperback)

978-1-77302-019-8 (ebook)

Published in Canada.

First Edition

Table of Contents

Preface

Since I started writing poetry in 1992 I have created many poems on a variety of different subjects. Many of my poems are from a Christian perspective, to give thanks and glory to my Lord and Saviour, Jesus Christ. God's design can be found everywhere if you open your eyes and quietly observe. Unlike my two previous books, this book is dedicated solely to Christian poetry. I would like to thank God for having an awesome family: my parents (Henry and Margaret) along with my brother Randy and his family. Without my dear friends, life would be a dreary, cloudy existence. I think that from Grande Prairie the list should include: Neil, Peter, John and Carl. Special mention included to Traci S. from Texas. Many of my poems are a modern version/interpretation of parables from the four Gospels. As I have been gifted with the knack of writing I hope that my work will be maximized for God's will in my life and that the reader will enjoy and ponder the poetry written within these pages.

February 26th, 2016

Quinn Graw

Acknowledgments Page

I would like to acknowledge and thank Coila Evans, a talented artist from Roundup, MT, for her permission to use the lovely drawing of the ichthys (fish symbol) on the back cover of this book.

Before Your Time

At a point in your life
The moment of realization perhaps arrives at once
That the stuff we own means as much
like a stack of wooden nickels
no matter how many pickles that huge jar can hold.
Before our time
When will we know the moment?
Our numbered days come to an abrupt end.
Have you said I love you or I'm sorry
to the ones whom you truly love?
Have you made amends with an estranged friend
or neighbour?
No guarantee one will live to an older age
When that day, year, month or hour sounds for the
final time
The voyage on Earth screeches to a halt on a dime.
Each of us exists until the appointed moment.
Before our time
how can we know?
when the hourglass runs out permanently.
Plan to live to be a hundred
if today contains your last breath then live it fully.
I hear that saying all the time

In the coffee shop from a farmer down the grapevine.
Maybe someone your own age bought the farm.
We say it is much too soon in our finite human terms.
Be aware you may be called next at any time.
The clock keeps ticking on your life.
Neither money or any stuff will be a lasting
legacy compared
to how you interacted with friends, families
and neighbours
Did you leave a better world than it was before
you arrived?
One more important question to ask
Did you know Jesus as Lord?
Shining in your life
Before your time?

Calm Thy Soul

In the hour of my despair
let my heart turn to you O Lord.
Fear of failure haunts my soul
Fear of what men think of me
shadows my timid heart.
Rarely do these fears ever come to pass
as the hours in my mind race with wild thoughts.
Calm thy soul
In peace I pray to you as I sleep
because in the Lord that I trust
He will deliver me safely from the doubts.
In God and His Word I shall trust
Fear not what the flesh can do to me.
Calm thy soul
Let the love of Jesus overcome
the crashing waves of anger
among the sins of the natural spirit.
Walk on the calm surface of the Rock
Walk in faith and be secure in Him.
Calm thy soul
Casting all your cares onto the cross on Calvary
For He always cared for you first.
Praise you Lord

Send the reassurances of your love
that I fervently seek today
to bring calm onto thy soul.

Prayers of an Eccentric Poet

My hope is in Jesus
where can I rediscover you?
I have not obeyed you now
My choices go awry and remain always dissatisfied.
Why God am I here?
Forgive my impertinence
Please do not be angry with my impatience.
No pleasure thrives in my existence.
Change my actions, then my heart
Perhaps vice versa is what I shall do.
Repentance I think is the proper course.
Forgive me Lord
Let me delve into your Word
I pray to you through these words
tumbling onto the written page.
Although Lord you know my thoughts
Before they come to attention in my mind.
I feel useless God
Is this despair what I write now?
Is it true what I feel is so real
Otherwise another lie I swallowed once again.
Show me my heart
I don't want to be here.

Failure and lack of persistence
Bely my failing strength.
I recall your grace and favours
for your reason I am one of your chosen flavours
in the rainbow of humanity
through the ultimate sacrifice
your holy name is given all the glory.
Praise you Lord Jesus
Thank you for your glory and bounty
On the cross at Calvary
I must acknowledge you on a bended knee.
As one of your many creations
For whom You said was created wonderfully
Thank you for listening
To the prayers of an eccentric poet.

The Psalm

Living in the moment
Dying inside this cubicle of time
What kind of psalm is this now?
How not to live
dissatisfied with everything one owns.
Selfish to the core
there must be more to life.
Deny oneself to the immediate time
Service must come to the forefront right now.

I struggle with the Word with no success.
Indifference, pride and gluttony are my adversaries.
Let there be peace in the soul.
Stop being black as coal in my brain
Wild outrageous thoughts plague the mind
the daily pattern repeats itself
lacking willpower and faith but especially love.

Trust in the Lord
so wake up my slumbering soul
Drawn in by his glory
to discover a meaningful life.
Succumb to the peace He offers.

Lose your life obtain an eternal bounty to gain.
This psalm I write, play and pray for you
for a praiseworthy life in your sight indeed.

Grace of Mercy

Stretch out the boundaries beyond your comfort zone.
follow the Lord living out his Word for harmoni-
ous accord.
Impatience and anger should be forgotten
for perfection you cannot achieve
without the grace of mercy at Calvary.
The nails piercing His hands and feet
contain for every person who has ever lived
the sins of unfaithfulness accumulated in store.
On the most decisive day of history
He bled your sins away with His blood.
V-day displayed God's vivacious love
Victory for the ultimate sacrifice and blessing He gave
to us.
Let the grace of mercy shroud our lives in love.
Do not be bitter or alone
for you cannot be cloned
Christ died for you at Calvary.
Three days hence
the tomb remained empty.
As He rose again defeating our sins of death
in the miracle of history known as Easter.
The disciples rejoiced

as even Thomas with the gift he received
In eyesight he saw his Lord and believed.

A long line of generations have lived and died
The immense Body of Christ has an innumerable sea
of souls
Awaiting the final conquest while residing in heaven.
When Christ comes to collect His bride
How many shall He find ready
For those welcoming Him with open arms.
you accept the grace of His gift of mercy.

Praise Him / Praise Hymn

Praise Him for my sight.
Praise Him for my taste buds.
Praise Him for my ability to walk and talk.
Praise Him for clean water to drink.
Praise Him I have plenty to eat.

Praise Him for my parents.
Praise Him for my brother and his family.
Praise Him for my friends.
few in quantity but gems in abundance.
Praise Jesus for my health.
Praise Him for the thorns of depression.
Praise Him for days that don't go well.
sing a praise hymn
relying on His will and not mine.
In your presence I need to dwell and stay.
Praise Him while learning patience and long-suffer-
ing kindnesses.

Let this be a praise hymn
every day begin to praise Him
when life begins to turn sideways
Remember to glorify Jesus

While returning home to His dwelling
for when we say Praise Him
may the kingdom consider this our praise hymn.

Lukewarm

The danger of apostasy looms
white is black and up is down
there is too much of what is wrong
like a virus spreading in this world we live in.
The condoning and acceptance of evil
the persecution of the believers
continues without a break
in Christ how many will hold on to the truth?
hanging on to His word
serving faithfully under duress.
Comfort and lukewarm apathy
mortal blows to one's faith.
Lax moral values sliding this society into oblivion.
What was written as sin
glorified as a relative truth
in today's modern society has gone amok
Do not be lukewarm but strong in faith
either hot or cold is preferable
to a wishy-washy state of mind.

The Unknown Cosmos

The vast immensity of the blackness in outer space
appears filled with a visual nothing.
while punctuated by the illusion of density.
Supernovae, black holes stars and quasars exist too.
Vast chasms of distances spread out the celestial wonders
revealing an immeasurable quantity measured in
light years
Dark matter and energy rule the universe.
Everything looks crowded
through the lens of the Hubble telescope.
Majestic explosions occurring eons ago
only now we see through the Earth's atmosphere and sky.
Can you measure God himself?
while His enormous universal playground staggers
the mind
via the length, width and depth.
So little visible to the naked eye
describing the multi-dimensions
we record knowledge through computer aided machines

What have discovered up to now
the mere tip of the iceberg.
What lies in the cosmos to be found?
new sciences will clash with old ideas
old thesis replaced by radical new hypothesis
The expansion of our knowledge
one day will blow our minds away.
The known Creator is unveiled by piecemeal
Shrouds of a knowledge curtain are pulled back bit by bit
Opening up a new can of worms to research.
One answered question reveals a hundred
new possibilities
the first step in finding order
begins as the first step in
discovering the divine order in the unknown cosmos.

Holding Tight

Let there be the Rock
when the storm starts raining hold on tight.
Let go of the junk food lifestyle
do not choose the flashy and the easy way.
Keep your eyes steady on the cross
hold on tight when the ship hits the rough seas.

Take refuge in the Rock
in Jesus your blessed savior.
Follow His Way as he preached and lived
Following Him, living without regrets.

In the good times be humble and praise him
do not surf the emotional waves
tossing to and fro as unstable and unready.
I always fail never measuring up
Lord show me your presence
holding you Jesus tight.
there is no other way
empty words without action is zilch
follow through with the good intentions
Hang on to the rainbow in the storm
the Rock will be holding tight unto you.

The Whispers of Peace

The wonderful breeze cools the skin
as the amazing beauty of sunlight
shines down upon God's wildlife.
Bless your heavenly Father tonight
stay happy and productive in your work.
For all creatures show them love galore
Be calm in this favourite site tonight.

Write a few words to everyone
display your talents to the crowd for a good purpose
as the whispers of peace blend into the wind.
God's voice is quiet
clear to hear
by opening our eyes and ears to ponder.
Stay calm keeping your feet grounded
during the busyness of life.
Let the traffic flow of worries pass on by
while the summer growth brings maturity
may the whispers of peace guide you today
the cool breeze of steady serenity
holds the forward path steady.

A Grand Day of Peace

Be grateful while walking with style
do not speak nor act two-faced.
Serve God as your Lord
If you forget Jesus in your heart
Practice what you believe now
for intellectual theology alone remains wanting
if you forget Jesus in your heart.
Read the Word
do not forget His name
neither in the good or the bad times.
Pray and call upon His name
by obedience in word and deed.
While in the garden of life
let the Lord prune your spiritual weeds.

Beauty of the weeds by smell and appearance
nevertheless a curse to the Lord.
Wean yourself away from the evil weeds
change your path and do not give in to apathy
Keep moving forward in faith
by fervent prayers on your knees
let Him answer each question with a guided answer.

Remember your first faith
the joy of salvation so dear
showing the peace in your heart like a gentle
calming breeze
Remember this while struggling day by day
emotions can mightily deceive
the rocky road that causes you to stumble.
Praise the Lord
You are worthy
the Son of God shining down His light at Calvary.
Hang on to Him
the world we know will disappear
trials and tribulations will beset all
many will grow faint and fail
as a precious few will persevere
the glory of God will be shown to those
faithful until the real end.
Thank you Jesus
for what you took away.
All the sin and fear now gone.

One day we will live in a wonderful peace with Jesus.
An eternal bounty of worship soon begins.
In discovering His true nature
we will find our true desires
matching perfectly with His will for our future lives.

Soon a grand day of peace
marking the greatest beginning of human history
well herald the start of the newest chapter.

The probing of the curious unknown of God's kingdom
will begin.
The forever story of God and man
once lost but now united for all time
this is the essence of a grand day of peace.

Emotions

Do you ever feel sanguine
overcoming a dark passage to cry and whine.
The clock winds down once again
emotions running high going around the bend at
high speed.
How you control feelings
when things go astray like a broken wheel
determine if another rim falls out of place.
More events occur turning into a blur of swirl-
ing thoughts.
Channel the passion inside the soul
restrain the negative thoughts in reality come to
pass rarely.
Smile in your mind and beam when you work
one man not overwhelmed by an emotional tidal wave
gains an unseen yet great victory.
The conquest over an impulsive anger rampage
a greater feat than any battlefield conquest.
Envy, malice, hopelessness
sadness, depression and hatred
brew together a bubbling cauldron galore.
Simmer down the tongue's inferno
pray and meditate to God for a sense of balance.

With a variety of emotions to choose from today
do not let untamed or unchecked feelings run wild at all.

Summer Evening

On a muggy and humid night in July
a warm breeze gently sways and tickles the leaves
as the sunshine blazes through the lovely trees.
The idyllic summer evening is now here.
The traffic flows on the highway steady
the background stream of noise drones constantly.
Saskatoon pie in the oven
I think the neighbours ought to be coming.
The heat of the working day fades
tailing off into a cooler temperature of this tranquil view
showing off the beauty of an enchanted summer evening.

Praise be to Jesus
the Son of God
Creator of the universe.
A clear blue sky a sign of peace
for this speaking breeze
bringing forth the sense
of how God created this Earth.
The creations of nature praise
to glorify His never-ending majesty.
The beautiful flowers blossom
the garden producing a bounty

of potatoes, radishes and lettuce.
Pine cones lie abound on the ground
many trees and shrubs exist to admire
Thank you God
for your grace and favour upon humanity
in the kindness of this summer evening.

Peacefulness of the Wind

Under the shade of the lush garden and the trees
a hymnal of the leaves
sing the chorus in the breeze.
Light or strong
with or without sunlight
the coolness refreshes
the days of summer.

Saskatoons grow in abundance
potatoes develop above,
yet produce underneath the hills
lettuce, carrots and peas
ripe for the picking
in the peacefulness of the wind.

The tender voice of God
whispers His intentions to us
we can hear
by opening our mind
and meditating with a closed mouth.
In the winter a chilling cold to the bone
in the summer a relief from the heat.
Listen with care and patience

the simple silence is an undervalued sound.
In a world of crowded noises surrounding us,
we often forget is the simple peacefulness in the wind.

Potato Snatcher

In the middle of a frosty October night
the passing traffic whispered as a quiet blip
the silence in the garden patch growing.
First the deer and coyotes snuck in
munching and digging up the carrots.
Wildlife arrived for easy meals
a booming shotgun blast chased them varmints away.

A single hill vanishes but the following night
a new potato hill emerges there.
Even after harvesting a row of reds and whites
there arrives another hill freshly bloomed,
the contents vanishing again without a trace.
One evening while sitting on the deck
as the sunset went down between the trees
in my mind these pondering thoughts swirled
and stormed.
Who was this potato snatcher?

Disappearing about this time one hill then another
I picked up one hill of potatoes
then another one popped up empty and still freshly dug.
No more potatoes for winter came a thought

as I watched and waited this night.
Dozing off I woke to the fright of a bright glaring light.
An imposing angel grimaced at me when I saw him.
"You have plenty while most people have nothing," the
angel stated.
Beware of the parable in the scriptures
about the rich farmer and his full barn
coming to naught while losing his life
as others took away what he had sown.
The angel's expression softened slightly
"I know your heart as does the Father.
Return to the fold and show your love for the Lord."

After this the angel vanished
as I pondered throughout the night
both through fretful thoughts and dreams.
when the next dawn broke
loading up the car with spuds
I gave a few potatoes to the homeless
asking around to nearby friends and neighbours
while unloading storage containers of spuds
to each neighbourhood without pause.
Finding carrots, onions and peas in the garden,
swiftly these were added to the care packages
to every family an anonymous note of blessing
placed alongside the container of potatoes.
After an exhausting day
I flopped into bed satisfied,
resting in peace for the first time in a month.

Waking up I thought I noticed
new potato plants ready to harvest.
Puzzled by this I dug out the potatoes
unloading and delivering invisibly to the recipients.
while touched by their predicaments of different kinds.
by the time I came home
the garden patch was bountiful again in full bloom.

Tomatoes, cabbages, pumpkins and cucumbers
scrawny before but a complete bounty of flawless
crops now.
I loaded these vegetables as I placed pails
beside the spuds to fill up for the next shipment to town.
In the morning one shared the veggies
with those in need getting the most
the potatoes now being shipped first to local neighbours
then nearby towns as well.
Another night arrived
yet an exhausted man was agog at the sight.
The garden was full
yet an extra row of potatoes appeared
after awhile this man dozed off again to be woken up
by the light of the same angel.
"Bless you," said the smiling heavenly host.
"The angel of death has passed
while in the previous four nights you have given away
all in your barns
all in your garden to the Father."
This man shook his head but the angel added,
"Listen to me for now from the poor and homeless

you have learned compassion and generosity.
No one in your town was without
even the most timid came to eat."
I gazed at him as he nodded.
"Tonight the town would have plundered
and trampled your garden.
yet unlike the parable
you humbled yourself first
then met the needs of your neighbours
in doing so you have fed the Son and honoured
the Father.
The potato snatcher as you say,
remains the soul catcher that
embraces the man who finally found
bountiful love and holy delight."
The angel suddenly vanished
I went to bed nervous but with an untold peace.
The next day the gardens and crops were so heavy
I hired every available man and woman standing
to harvest.
All of the barns and granaries were filled in this area
that the town built more barns and granaries in reserve
for there was another dream coming to mind
showing seven years of famine to come after one year
of bounty.
One night I bowed my head
as the community worshipped together
Both the potato snatcher and soul catcher
My king now owned my entire heart
as what He desired for so long has come to pass.

More potatoes to be snatched and harvested
in that moment I realized that time is against us
to harvest not potatoes but souls.
The finality of His imminent return
shows us the narrow path of eternal freedom.
It is time to bring the potatoes home.

What Do You Worship?

Everyone has a goal
Everybody spends their life in a different way.
Man is a spiritual being designed to worship God
yet man chooses from many other paths today.
What do you worship?
Is it junk food or is it Facebook on your phone?
some worship television, some worship reading
in our life who do we worship?
Do we bow down to money, job or our family?
Who created the universe and all that is in it?
some worship the trees and the creations
paying little attention to the Creator.
Is it possible that Jesus is the Son of God?
He wants followers not fans
Jesus died on the cross on Calvary
He rose from the dead three days later
removing the sting of death from humanity.
Jesus let me worship you
allow all men and women to worship you as well.
What or who do you worship?
the Son of God knocks on your heart
open the door and let Him in to take control.
Let Him mould every aspect of your life
to shine like Him in this darkened world.

Abide in Jesus

Shout out His name
be joyous in the presence of the Lord.
Abide in Jesus
I struggle so
it is a hard and narrow path
Time is short for humanity
we all run out of time too quickly.
Rely not on the waves of emotion
but a steady faith that hangs upon Jesus.
He saved us on Calvary
cling to God and serve Him
Let us abide in Jesus
each one finds the Lord for salvation
serving Him as faithfully as we can.
Find friends who are believers
cherish and learn from one another
encourage and love as sisters and brothers
while continuing to abide in Jesus today.

Thoughts in Church

Do people worry about their jobs?
Perhaps not wanting to talk to that fellow
who looks like a slob sitting in the same pew.
While in the church service
how many are distracted?
like why am I here
or this building sure is showing its age.
I wonder about the cross
many colours and shades are on display
in jewelry of all sorts today.
The meaning of the cross
in the world is diluted
as a status symbol it is polluted.
being crucified a horrible way to die
in the ancient society for the lower classes.
We have lost the cost
upon His death at Calvary.
Have I digressed about thoughts in church?
During the hymns do we worship
or teem with impatience to get this over with?
Do we think about families, the car,
the spouse or about the big game?
Keep your eyes on Jesus

it should be a lifetime goal
not a struggle for an hour and a half
on every morning of Sunday.
Stay awake
be willing to grow your faith
to stand up and believe when the time is needed.

Have I Told You Lately?

Have I told you lately?
How have I shown you?
You are my King
by my actions, words and thoughts
that you are the Every Thing.
I keep failing you
What have I lost
to follow you Lord?
You paid the steepest cost on the cross
Sacrifice the idols that are obstacles
knock down the barriers that keep you out
let my heart be pure and stout.
Have I displayed my loyalty Jesus?
Like Peter how many times have I denied you?
Thank you Lord for being my Creator
Everything exists because of you
Praise to you my King
you are my everything.
Have I told you lately?
Worshipping you with my heart
for nothing I do on my own
remains worthy of a hill of beans
compared to what you did on Calvary.

Crucified like the lower class criminals
Nailed to the cross
both hands and feet pierced
a spear through your side.
The land quaked
the sky turned dark and black.
while the heavens were rocked
by your sacrifice Lord Jesus
Have I told you lately?
Have I shown others today?
what you told me
when three days later
an angel appeared at your grave
announcing your resurrection
to the faithful and to the disciples
the fulfillment of a divine insurrection.
Son of God worthy of praise
Holiness worthy of eternal worship
each person should say
Thank you Jesus for being who You are
being pure and righteous and loving
demanding all from the true follower.
Like the parable of the woman
giving the single coin all that she had
or the woman who worshipped Him
pouring expensive perfume on his head.
Giving their everything
because they were forgiven much
each of them gave themselves to Jesus
written in the Bible their deeds remembered always.

Have I told you lately?
I love you Jesus
All around me there are people to pray for
needs and hurts stack above the highest ground
Let me pray for those nearest
remind me Lord every one of us is your dearest.
Praise to you King of Kings
today, tomorrow and forevermore
let us worship the King
letting our lives be on display
saying I love you Jesus.

Twist of Fate or God

In a game of life
one side may be winning
as the final quarter winds down
yet the trailing team marches down the field.
In the failing seconds
at the one yard line
a surprise move with a final pass
intercepted creating turmoil in the ensuing mess.
Twist of fate or God
sometimes we march down the field
conquering our goals, we move forward
then inexplicably we toss an interception
perhaps fumbling the ball to frustrate our labour.
God is in control
to get our attention
He has to knock us down
Is this a twist of fate?
When we have a flat tire on a trip
or have a bad day at work
plans falling through we were counting on
Is that fate or a twist from God?
Look around you now
Are you being pursued?

I'm afraid to turn around in fear
I think I'm too late to go back to Him.
Don't let lies stand in the way
Remember Him
let his light
chase the darkness away.
is it a twist of fate?
or a twist from God
an invitation desiring for you to come to Him.
Humble your heart
be kind to others
let the light of the Lord
shine upon the night surrounding you.
Like a moth to the flame
who will see Him through you?
Let a twist of God
bring you to the knees of prayer
in the name of Jesus say Amen.

Friendly Takeover

Is there a better time
for learning new verses, taking them to heart?
Share your whole heart with Jesus
let Him make a friendly takeover.
No demands, no bargaining
just unconditional surrender
make Christ the CEO of your life.
Love Him more than your own self
allow your desires to die daily
When you morph into who God wants you to be
then you will discover the true self
you have always desired to be.
Hug closely to God
hold on as the winds of change blow.
Stay true to your faith
allow the Potter to mold you.
It is not painless yielding to the purge of sins
follow His footsteps just ahead of you
Thank you Jesus
for your undying mercy.
Show me your presence
for tonight my heart is sinking deep
yet I praise you Jesus

for you are the grace and favour
the Rock is the essence of life
Nothing moves without your knowledge.
Salvation is meant to be a friendly takeover.
no hostile takeover
no one setting rules forcing you to live by.
Hand over the controls to the Lord
steer the course as God sees fit
into the fog of the future only Jesus knows.
I feel the need
as does everyone who knows
to let Him run my life
as I've failed every way in every day.
Give worthy praise and worship to Jesus
for only He understands and knows.
He lived perfectly as one of us
not sinning while showing us
how to follow Him.
A friendly takeover
that is the ultimate bargain.
We give Him our sins at Calvary
yet as we turn our heart to match with him
we become part of His family
an eternal place of residence to worship in heaven.
How could you or I ignore
such a business proposition?
A stiff price against selfishness
yet the greatest deal for us is a friendly takeover
a free gift extended out
from the eternal God who loves us so.

The Sadness Song

My eyes have strayed from you
when I am filled with the sadness song.
Praise be to you Jesus
Good Shepherd and King of Kings.
I stumble seeking your way on a rocky path
as the feet get sore and the spirit grows weary
then the heart plays the sadness song.
The cross at Calvary I remember
how could I ever forget your great sacrifice?
Raise my soul
let me be a light to others
first at home then at work.
Smile with your tender heart
remove this sadness
replace it with your shining glory to always remain there.
You are worthy of great praise
let me serve you
as I pray now and throughout the day.
Praying for other people's concerns
one grows closer to you Lord
Let the song of grace and peace
bring forth the joy from you Jesus.
Praise you forevermore

one day I will be on my knees
when I meet you on the first day of eternity.
Let your love be in my heart
to daily carry the cross for you.
I thank you Lord for sharing
opening my eyes
to the errors of my ways as I fail too often.
let my thoughts be with you
forgetting the negative and evil plans
thwart and remove them from my mind.
Let the song of sadness go
allow the flow of peace into our hearts.
Forget the fumbles of yesterday
be focused on today
trusting the future in His hands.
Dark clouds do not remain forever
as the sunlight first peeks
through the clouds of trials and tribulations
then the rays beam down on us with the warmth of love.
The song of sadness
now sang as the song of our gratitude.

Mosaic of the Messiah

There are so many aspects Lord
an infinite variety of characteristics describing your Son.
Jesus is love He is forgiveness
Protector, righteous, perfect
He is sinless though he was tempted as we are.
The mosaic of the Messiah
an endless list of descriptions for him.
Humble yet our holy Judge
Strong and courageous
each word fitting into the puzzle
revealing to those who seek His face
as the mosaic of the Messiah is revealed
yet never ending in discoveries of his nature.
Friend and teacher yet so much more
Abba, my Father is one more trait to adore.
Each description is interpreted throughout eternity
Lord and King, El Shaddai, Saviour of mankind
Creator of space and the universe
Inventor and designer of planet Earth
Fun, joy and happiness all part of His nature.
Jealous of His name
Christ the healer his ultimate goal
bringing back the human race to the Father.

Good Shepherd tending the flock
Wisdom and hope He wants to share
while rescuing so many lost lambs.
Jesus is all of the above
yet so much more while trying to decipher
the full mosaic of the eternal Messiah.

Lost and Found

On a frosty spring morning
snowflakes flurry above in the air
covering for one last time
a thin white blanket on the sidewalk
the leftovers from yesterday's storm.
The streets exist as empty paths
very few walk about on a Sunday morning.
Some people go to the coffee shop
the place for the lonely
a stopping spot for the lost and found.
Despite keeping up appearances
many lost sheep wander in our society.
All different folks yet would we be surprised
who is lost but not yet found?
One out of a hundred the lost sheep
wandering in the wilderness
pursued by the Shepherd
relentlessly without fatigue or disinterest.
This sheep will hear the Shepherd and obey.
What celebrations will take place
as the Shepherd throws the greatest party.
Ninety nine celebrate alongside Him
as the heavens rejoice

over the one sheep
finding the way back to the flock.
The lost and found
surround us every day.
Worship the King
serve others with compassion.
Let the dove of peace
shine brightly to the lost
pointing the way to finding the Shepherd
waiting with open arms extended
to celebrate one more soul coming home.

The Vineyard

In a small rural town
the economy was depressed with jobs being
sparsely available.
Hope was a rare and difficult commodity to find
in the cloud of gloom and doom hanging overhead.
One day a wealthy businessman came to town.
Deciding to build a vineyard, he bought a field.
He drove to town just before nine a.m.
finding shiny SUVs and brand new trucks at
a restaurant.
Then he walked up to find the place full
men and women in business suits idly chatting away.
"Why are you people not working?" the man asked.
One man answered, "There is no work
our businesses are slack
as both the oil fields and the sawmill are shut down."
"Come and work in my vineyard
prepare the field for planting," the owner replied.
"I will pay you seventy dollars for the day
payment in cash at six o'clock to each of you."
The people agreed and so the vineyard owner
drove his bus to the front of the restaurant
hauling the people out to his field outside of town a ways.

The vineyard owner explained what he wanted to do
clearing the weeds and prepare the field for planting.
His workers began to work at nine a.m.
picking stones and removing weeds from the field
as the owner supervised the operation.
The owner envisioned the overwhelming task at hand
so at noon he drove back into town
noticing a lot of pickup trucks
parked in front of the same coffee shop since nine a.m.
Entering the café he noticed a lot of farmers chatting
so the vineyard owner asked what they were doing.
One farmer answered there is no work
no rain has fallen yet and the crops look bleak.
The vineyard owner offered the farmers
seventy dollars a day to be paid at six o'clock that night.
The farmers discussed the offer and agreed to work.
The owner brought the new help to join the other crew
who raised eyebrows at the farmers
yet continued to work alongside the new bunch.

At three o'clock the vineyard owner
saw the work was going quicker
but there was still an enormous job to do
so he drove the bus back to town.
He saw a number of people
standing outside the grocery store.
He saw they were retail workers
being let off for the day as there was not enough work.
The owner gave them the same offer
quickly the bus was filled

and there were more workers in the field.
The nine a.m. sweating workers grumbled
snapping orders at the retail workers
until the farmers glared the nine a.m. crew into silence.

Just before five o'clock
the first workers raised their eyebrows
as the vineyard owner drove to town for the last time
that day.
Stopping in front of the tavern
he found the local drunks, homeless and scoundrels.
They were soon arriving at the field at five p.m.
as the nine a.m. workers turned their noses up at them.

At six o'clock the owner beeped the horn on his bus.
The workers came over as he started to pay the workers.
First he paid the local drunks, the homeless and
the scoundrels
seventy dollars in cash eliciting mutterings from the nine
a.m. crew
Ignoring them the boss paid the retail workers and
the farmers
the same amount of seventy dollars.

Finally the nine a.m. crew arrived to be paid
murmuring and bickering about the other people who
hadn't worked
the full day and that they should be paid more than
the rest.
The owner paid them the full seventy dollars

and one of them complained about working the
whole day.
But the vineyard owner finally lost his patience.
"That's enough of the complaining," he snapped.
"I need many workers for this job
and who are you to say
how I shall spend my money?
Are you jealous of my generosity?
I've seen how you look down
at the farmers and the store workers,
but worse yet the poor, homeless and the drunks
that I brought in at five p.m.
The wage is the same for all
so that none may go hungry."
The nine a.m. crew gawked
as the vineyard owner softened his steel glance.
"Look at the fields to be planted and harvested.
Beware that the first shall be last
and that the last shall be first.
There is no other work around here
but you do not know the day and hour
that the job will be completed.
For surely the five p.m. workers will be first
then the three p.m. and the noon workers
will be called in for the final payday
as I shall issue equal share to all of the faithful
that they will each be an owner
sharing the bounty of this vineyard.
But to those who question my decisions
some you will find left out

not being called for the final payday.
As the others rejoice in the bounty
you will be gnashing your teeth with hunger pains
looking in from the outside upon my beautiful vineyard.

The Businessman and the Young Woman

In a rustic rural area there was a country church,
a resting place for tourists and locals alike.
The sun passed through the stain glass window
lighting up the wooden cross
beyond the altar hanging on the wall.
A young aboriginal woman
walked in and sat down on the front pew.
An older businessman came in
sitting down in the same pew.
The young woman was shabbily dressed
while the businessman wore a tailor made suit.
The young woman was in tears
and kept her head down
wondering how she was going to stop drinking
worrying about how she was going to pay the bills
as a single mom for her children
praying for mercy that she was not worthy of His love.
The businessman dismissed the woman as not being
like him.
He reminded God of the charities he supported
the tithes he made to his church
all of his good works in the community came to mind.

He prayed that his works would let others
be more like him and that the church would grow.
The cross began to shine in vibrant colours.
After some time both stopped praying
while gazing at the cross.
They both realized the other was there
as the young woman beamed with a wide smile at
the businessman
while he initially frowned but smiled back at her.
The young woman glowed with contentment when she
stood up
walking down the aisle as light as a bird.
while he mused about the lack of peace in his own heart.
The businessman felt no contentment or grace
as he was still the same man as before.
He stood up as the sun fell off the cross
in that old country church.
Walking down the aisle
he felt his legs move like concrete.
Slipping out onto the church entrance
he noticed the young woman hopping and dancing
as one of her friends waited for her
in the gravel parking lot inside a brown used car.
The businessman saw them drive away
while he sat on a bench nearby.
For the first time in his life
he cried and wept
as his thoughts pondered
on realizing what he had become
and what he had missed out on life.

The Easter Miracle

As the blood flowed freely from the cross
two thousand years ago
the history of mankind is transformed forever
unveiling the ultimate gift
to whoever chooses to accept the gift.

On the hill at Calvary
God fulfilled his promise for all to see.
His twelve followers fled the scene
one of them made a betrayal so obscene.

In his short earthly life Jesus healed the sick
bringing hope to the poor without a home of brick.
Humbling the stiff necked Pharisees
He sought to change the heart of humanity
changing their inner soul one at a time that was the start.
Then the outside will show the changes
displaying the growth of the new glowing peace.

Thirty pieces of silver was a pitiful sum
betraying the Messiah turned a soul so numb.
His followers were discouraged
seeing him whipped and scourged.

He was beaten to carry His own cross
until they arrived on the spot.
Nailed and hoisted upon the cross
when all appeared to be lost
God's victory became complete and final.
as the sky darkened and roared
the miracle of the moment soared
on the Earth and in the heavens.

Three days later the tomb was there
as the rock rolled away a few did stare.
An angel declared the victory
changing the course of mankind's future history.

Christ was crucified and died
He rose from the dead to be glorified.
The sting of death forever nullified
revealing to us all
the plans of our Abba Father
now permanently satisfied.

On this day we remember the Easter miracle
the blood He sacrificed on the cross
He made as a vow to us.
We must accept His ultimate gift
kneeling down to His will
then He will lift us up as children of heaven.
At Calvary when time stood still
we can go forth asking for a pardon of grace
that is God's desire and path for the human race.

The Persistent One

The lady judge arrived to the small town
for every two weeks she presided over local disputes.
A poor man came to her
pleading that he had not been paid
for over three months then dismissed by his former
cruel boss.
She had other cases before him
but never ruled in his case
even though he pleaded his case to her.
Month after month
from winter to spring this continued.
The judge was not particularly caring or just
for those in this community.
But she began to weary as the summer approached
as the man was not weary nor did quit his cause.
She wondered how he could persist
fearing he may sue her or harm her in another way.
Better to settle this matter now she thought
or no peace would ever come to me.
As the court day arrived this time
the poor man was the only one who showed up.
Summoning him in the front of the bench
she asked him to repeat his request.

He answered and repeated his case
but this time the judge hit her gavel down on her bench.
"I award you what you request
you shall be paid all of the back wages plus interest.
You have won your case."
The man thanked her and leapt into the air with joy
leaving the court humble with grateful, happy tears.
The judge pondered for a moment before thinking
out loud
"This was a persistent one who never gave up.
How better off would we all be if everyone pleaded
their case
so fervently without ceasing."

A Piece of Peace

A piece of peace
on occasion may flounder astray
Leave your heart open
to the sunshine of God's love.
Pray for all desires
both large and small
for friend and foe alike.
Commit to prayer without stopping
keep the communication line to God busy and hopping.
Today pray all day long
let your faith be strengthened to be strong.
Whether at home or at work
remember kindness and don't be a jerk.
Traffic rolls on by
as one walks on the path
the subtle wind warms the cool air
as spring has arrived.
The piece of peace shall grow
letting the grass and trees turn green
as the warmth of the sun melts the icy heart.
Stay outside and remain in the light
do not be afraid of the dark.
While traveling to work

ponder the cross
the missing piece for peace
that will be always fulfilled for the willing.
Thank you Jesus
Praise you for this new day
every moment, every breath
a gift from you
celebrating a piece of peace.

Sweet Salvation

O sweet salvation
I remember you back then
the calming peace I found in my soul
while waking up with Jesus
for the very first time.
Can I forget that day?
While finding your grace
so desperate not to be lost
I realized the highest cost
you paid for me Lord.
Now I need to tell someone
how much Christ means,
what he has done for me.
Thank you Jesus for not giving up
on a sinner drifting in the past
when forward thinking is needed instead.
Praise you God for this sweet salvation
Your words are meant to recall
buried and intertwined within the heart
the sweet salvation of that day.
Help me back to that precious day
when I was lost but found your righteous way.
Rediscover the oh sweet salvation

every day moving towards you Lord.
Speak and live in my life.
Praise you Jesus always for what you have done.
Erasing my sins
that were meant for me to bear.
Taking my place on the cross
removing my sinful stains by grace
the sweet salvation a gift for everyone.

The Sunset Begins

As I sit on the park bench
on a crisp, cool evening
the sunset arriving but not here yet
a chilly wind moves the dead leaves.
A contrast with the greenness of spring
not achieved at this moment.
I ponder the stealth
the quick passing of time and health
past the halfway mark in the journey of life.
One creates much ado about regrets and strife
Can I have a bit of a reprieve?
in the name of Jesus I believe
End times rushing toward us faster than ever before
Moral values dying out like the dinosaurs.
As the sunset begins
the light is bountiful still
as the routine of life daily dwindles.
let our love glow ablaze
never forgetting the promise to renew and rekindle
the gift which we cannot repay.
While the sunset begins
it ushers in an eternal dawn.

Spring Joy

The blessing of a slight breeze
in the cool spring evening
brings contentment to a weary day.
Both work and confusion
coexist with crankiness and a happiness infusion.

Contentment through godly thoughts
follow the Lord, be peaceful in your soul.
Let the confusion, anger and stress come to naught
peace without the idol of materialism is the goal.
I find tranquility in the written word
to share with others my gift
allowing God's work to shine through me
to encourage or inform someone I do not yet know.

Spring joy
let it not be so coy
it is hard to let frustration and confusion go
a decoy stopping the writing stream flow.
Let the name of a friend
perch in my thoughts
with the benefits of lovely memories
soothing and taming my wild impulses

to bring solidarity in soul and body.
Serving Jesus is the struggle
time to let go and muzzle ourselves
to Him we should cozy up and nuzzle.

His return is so near
we must love another
as Christ did so long ago on the cross.
Let the spring joy reign
seek neither fame or fortune
in the quietude of an evening of peace
be still to find the heart of God
urging you to merge your heart rate
from two discordant beats to a steady even pounding.

Haiku Praise

Without God I moan
without cash turn to Jesus
wealth beyond compare.

On Calvary cross
sacrifice of blood for us
conquest defeats sin.

Faithful friend from God
worth more than money or gold
Devote our love Lord.

Springtime brings new hope
lush grass, flowing rivers roar
fresh smells belong now.

Gloom & Doom

Excited imaginations fill my head
everyone plots against me with evil dread
More wicked thoughts swirl in my scattered brain.
Increased wilder thoughts emerge
the emotional waves crash up and down
like a raging sea storm.
throwing my soul into a resentful stew.
Let my anxiety submerge
as my virtues are far and few.
one keeps busy at work
my duties I did not shirk
while am underlying despair begins creeping in
by stealth it is a devious sin.
Failure is the norm
lack of success to society is an inability to conform.
I cannot control my thoughts
only by biting my tongue do they come to naught.
In this mood I see so clear
the vibrant grey blackness of life
that I have neglected in spades.
There is no rest for a malcontent
living on his own instead of God's will.
The slight breeze of a spring evening

amplifies the sadness squeezing around my throat.
Arrogant to think I am special
God creates us all in his image
by pitiful efforts I fail alone.
When the gloom and doom does lift
there is a noticeable life altitude shift
when I follow Him the spring in my step bounces spry.

State of Forgiveness

It is the state of forgiveness
the heavy stone of burdens now taken away.
My sins heavily laid me down
for who will there be a crown to adorn?

I am the lowest of the heart
with an arrogant attitude to start.
Humble me Lord to do some good
traveling for you in my neighbourhood.

Let your gifts be a bonus
to help the people nearest to one as the onus.
Let the materialistic vision gain a new focus
before I find myself in a local version
the unveiling of a plague of locusts.

Praise be to Jesus my King
it is time to unlock the heart to sing.
Genuine faith belies the fear
sincerity and willingness to obey is so clear.

A free pardon shall not be turned down
so get rid of that nasty lonely frown.

Everyone searches for meaning in life
pointing towards God
the Son shed His blood for every person.
Close the heart to the junk food of the world
then hang on to the rock while the wind swirls
the rock will keep you from being twirled
as the state of forgiveness begins right now.

Terraform the Heart

Is there terraforming happening in our hearts?
is a change of my attitude to serve others needed today?
Why are you miserable
unless you don't know God
the final measurement is so terrible and terrifying.
Do not be deceived
by concepts that man conceives.
Allow the transformation of the soul inside to occur
as the inner beauty blossoms
on the outside with smiling faces.
Let the cancer of self-absorption
die right alongside
the towering height of materialism run amok.

Change us for your glory Jesus.
In our mind and thoughts
let the heart and soul be yours.
Terraform the heart
praise you Jesus for everything
Open my eyes to the goodness you bring
let our soul daily sing praise to you.
A change of scenery
a different perspective to view

brings a radical change
when the heart is terraformed into His image.

The Rich Yuppie

When a middle aged pastor just finished the service
a few members of the congregation came forward
the man of God noticed once again
a well-off, young yuppie sitting
on the back pew for several Sundays.
The pastor beckoned the young man forward
and the man burst forth towards the altar
wearing his tailor made-to-fit suit
with a new tablet in his hand.
Arriving at the front the young man frowned
"Preacher man how do you get to heaven?
How does one know this invisible Jesus?" he blurted.
A few of the congregation bristled and muttered
but the preacher smiled raising his hand to silence
the murmurs.
"Young man have you followed the
Ten Commandments?"
"Yes sir. I can name them all too," answered the
young yuppie.
"That's fine son but I noticed that you were playing
with your tablet during the service. What were
you doing?"
The young man blushed then admitted,

"checking out the sports scores, the news, Facebook
and Twitter."
"You missed the message young man
I say that status and money have gone to your head.
Give up the tablet and let's say donate twenty thousand
to the new homeless shelter downtown.
Spend time serving others with love
if you really want to find Jesus."
The young yuppie shook his head
walking back down the aisle in disbelief.
By the time he arrived at his car
the tablet screen was turned back on.
At the altar one of the congregation asked
"Pastor why did you bother
talking to him knowing his reputation?"
The lost shall be found
although a camel walking through a needle is easier
than a rich man entering the kingdom of heaven.
After a few weeks while the service was nearly over
the pastor noticed the young yuppie arriving late.
Not having been there the past while
the pastor noticed something different
the young man was in tears with a fragile smile.
Interrupting the sermon the pastor startled every one
by dismissing the congregation a little early
Rushing down to the young yuppie
waiting for the congregation to empty out the pews.
"What is it my son?" he asked compassionately.
"It is like this preacher," the young man sniffed
"after what you said a few weeks back

I searched my heart and looked around me
finding expensive toys and trinkets not really satisfy-
ing me
trying to fill my heart but not succeeding.
"So I went down and donated forty thousand
as my heart dictated me to do
to build the new homeless shelter with thirty extra beds."
The pastor smiled and said,
"That is wonderful, but why are you in tears?"
"I downsized my house and my car,
giving to the poor and the women's shelter.
I prayed for guidance to come here to you
feeling an inner peace and joy that I haven't felt before.
What's happening to me preacher?
I feel transformed from the inside a kind of
new creature."
The pastor put his hand on his new brother.
"Come and let me buy you lunch
as you have humbled yourself.
Salvation has come to you young man
For you have found Jesus in your heart.
He was always waiting for you to repent
now you are a truly rich man in eternal treasures."

The Ingrate

The confident young executive
strode into the boardroom,
an icy chill filling the atmosphere
with the shareholders and CEO glaring at him.
Sit down Peters, grumbled the CEO
we have got a serious matter to discuss.
The young man frowned as he pondered his plight.
Yes I'm talking about the financial irregularities
with regards to the McGregor account.
The youngster began opening his mouth
but was cut short by the CEO.
I could fire you and lay charges against you.
Fifty thousand missing from the account
set up by your shady friend.
Glancing at the frowning shareholders
the CEO startled the young man
getting out of the chair to shake Peters hand.
Even though almost everybody wants you canned,
I still believe in you.
But for one year you will be on strict probation.
Just remember to pass along the favour,
moral ethics are not a monthly flavor.
The young man Peters left the room chagrined

upset by the accusation
angered by the thought
who had tipped off the big cheese?
Here he was, the bee's knees
dressed down in front of the board.
Three days later
Peters scoured the internal networks
finding a discovery that made him incensed.

Entering his protégé McPherson's cubicle stall
he interrupted the colleagues online off of Skype.
Listen here McPherson
I know the little scam you pulled
a five thousand dollar vacation
that you lulled out of the PR department

now it is time to pay it back
or lose your apartment.
Mcpherson begged for more time
but Peters wouldn't allow him out
without paying back the very last dime back.

Security came and hauled McPherson out
but his colleagues were furious and stout
Peters walked away proud for flexing his clout.
Mcpherson's friends left in a hurry away
to the CEO they bled their fury
then Peters was summoned to another meeting.
The CEO was alone with the coworkers
some security and a police officer in tow.

The CEO growled at Peters,
You wicked ingrate
I forgave you for the fifty thousand debt
but now I hear you turfed McPherson who wept
Five thousand you wouldn't forgive or forget
but now that will be your regret.
You are fired now
Mcpherson will have your job.
I'm having you arrested right now
as the furious CEO shook his head.
You will not get out of jail without fail
unless you pay back every cent
that you have foolishly misspent.
Peters the ingrate
realized his errors too late
as he was escorted towards
a lengthy prison date.

The Follower's Price

Today do not let neither be
any hardship under the sea
on the land or flying in the air be
from keeping one separated from God's care.
Neither a job loss or a friend who deserts
take away an incalculable treasure that is wise.
An economic calamity could befriend
as self-reliance disappears and flies.
Do not gamble in the pleasures of dice
this a key element in the follower's price.

Avoid allowing the grief of death
to gain a foothold in one's soul
do not allow the dead to make you deaf to Jesus.
Avoid living as a lump of black coal.
The past come and gone and the future lies ahead
be prudent, plan to live in today's moment.
Dwelling on the pain what you already see
rehashing events is the opposite of obedience.
a key element to recover
in the follower's price
one must daily discover the faith.

Yet a third element exists in store,
not what you own or purchase online.
With family ties closely knit to the core
the distraction to service is beyond a byline
Family sometimes diverts the attention of one
distracting our eyes off the heavenly Son.
It is good for family to be together
like a flock of birds with similar feathers.
One cannot look back while plowing a field
otherwise a worthless path will be revealed.
Keep your open eyes straight ahead
on the hill lies the path
to the cross that you must tread.
File daily concerns and materialistic distractions
out of your mind
as the follower's price is a numbing grind.
every daily choice for Jesus to us does remind
that the follower's price is so
finding and binding closer to Him
so one does not become spiritually blind.

Giving

Does it matter much
what the TV preachers ask to give?
God is infinitely more than a pledge of money.
He asks you to serve right where you are.
Life can be like an abundance of honey
otherwise it's like driving a broken down car.
Whether it is your time, talents or resources
give to God the entire abundance.
Move beyond the comfort zone
while standing on a ledge all alone.
Let your faith grow and blossom
do not try to hide like a possum.
When confessing your sins
provide others with your ample blessings.
Jesus owns it all anyhow
so let your two copper coins take a bow.
Serve with generosity
live God's life with a passionate ferocity.
A lesson learned here today
to give your life whole heartedly
in many different ways.

Give as you are given
without any half-hearted tries
live a full life without lies.

Thoughts of the Heart

Black poplar, spruce and the pine
every species owns needles and leaves in its own time.
The spring life and renewed green colour
with the chirping chats among the birds
sing in harmony with the frogs singing from afar.
different reasons for different seasons in life
as every person contains
a rich variety of emotions in store.
sometimes calm and content
sometimes pining for more.
Be content with what you possess
many people don't have food
not alone possessions worth much less.
Time to tinker with the thoughts of the heart
turn ideas on their head to see how you are blessed.
Wisdom is obedience to God.
look at the land and the crops being sown in the sod.
The crops bloom and steadily rise above the stubble
as existing lodgers this planet is a
miraculous creative bubble.
Let the gentle cool breeze
temper the impatience
wild emotions riding like a roller coaster

within the thoughts of the heart.
Smile and let love enter
do not allow sour, envy and malice
to be the soul's renter.
Give thanks and credit due
for the variety of life that we view.
We are not owners but passing renters.
Let us learn the lesson
to be lenders and not grabbers
The world does not rotate around anyone named ME.
while Jesus is on display to behold for free.
The galaxies are a wonder so far from here
let the thoughts of the heart be of good cheer
as Jesus is on a beholden display for free.

Hard Days

Struggling while hanging on to the rope
on those days do not let your feelings elope.
On those hard days when your soul is low
Say no to the spirits from below
avoid the demons from gaining a foothold.
Let your faith grow
without tossing about like a high wave on the sea.
Allow perseverance and love to sow
Lean on Him strong
steering your thoughts from going wrong.
Praise Him in song
Avoid the trap of believing you are a loser
Do not be to others a bruiser.
Hold on to Jesus today
Weak of faith I may be
When the hard days come
let me stay on the Rock
do not drive around the block searching for better days.

Grow and bloom from the hard days
Learn to walk His way
Step by step
as He will keep you safe and kept.

Peace Through Prayer

Instead of indulging self-serving thoughts
think about a neighbour or friend in need
Plant a kernel of prayer as seed.
Do not allow weeds to choke out the sunlight.
Prune and burn the branches to let your light shine.
peace through prayer brings a calm delight.
Be steady and wait on Him
for you shall be fine.
Worrying doesn't add a centimeter to your height
so dial while on your knees
Heaven the ultimate social media eternal hotline.
Acquire his knowledge out of the Bible
store it in your heart where He always sees.
Check your purposes and the reasons
why you do something
remains just as important as what you do.
Humble prayer is the ultimate power
Let the Lord be your guidance tower
to be faithful and true do not cower.
Peace through prayer is the spiritual glue
to hold the life boat together
not to be swept up by the choppy waves of life.
You may feel blue

as He chips away your rough spots
with the precision of the surgical scalpel knife.
Praise God in all times
exceptionally difficult where there is no reason or rhyme.
Daily and hourly reassurance is not a dare.
So send to Him every care
big or small upwards on heaven's ladder
the salvation of the soul is what matters
by the means of peace through prayer.

Edge of Paradise

On this spring evening tonight
emerges a perfect alignment of the sun and a breeze
as a gentle touch soothes the heating blaze.
Planting flowers display one of God's delights
soon we will no longer fear the breeze.
No more business today
as we dwell in the Lord's maze.
Tonight I feel the edge of paradise
seeing a subtle glance into eternal treasures.
Peace and calm dwell in the cool wind
a foreshadowing of heaven as a splice
to this dying world a worthy measure
a future glory that our hopes are pinned.
Praise you Jesus
the breeze has stopped for a second
as birds chirp while flying by.
Solitude with the sunset at my back is a real wow.
Even as the sounds of passing traffic beckon
the edge of paradise asks why?
listen to the quietude of the voice of God
speaking in the whispers of leaves
Stay still and believe
allow the grace of God to surround you,

while relaxing and dwelling in the Lord
In the miracle of creation
take a back seat to relax and observe
the works of the Creator who deserves
on the edge of paradise to be served.

Is There a God of Peace?

In this world we live in now
a calming presence versus the expensive lease
To which God do we bow down to now
the god of mammon and possessions
do you pay homage to Jesus in his royal processions?
The rising sun in the clear blue sky
singing birds with the chattering nature
wake up all of His nomenclatures
Today in stride we walk
Whom do we stalk or is it money?
A symphony of songs
ring out from a flock of local birds
chirping and chattering as a flying herd
Ducks and geese add their calls
to the bird chat I hear from near and afar
In the silence of the morning
the quiet of the evening pervades the air
one can sense the awesome presence
even among the chaos of human life
the presence of the God of peace.

Believe in Him

When your heart is black
once more grumpy and complaining
remember God whose heart is paining.
Compared to India I do not lack
even in the current job
one is not part of a vast unemployed mob.
So many have lost hope
without family or friends to cope.
Remember Jesus in gratitude
change the latitude of your attitude
Believe in Jesus right now
hold on to your faith to make it strong
in bad times do not have a cow
when the day goes sour will be
for you never know when will be your final hour.

Believe in Jesus
humble yourself as a tool
let me Lord be your humble fool
bringing others closer to you
so stop fretting in a stew.
The sun still shines
don't let your heart go blind

in nature you find God everywhere
the word of the Lord shows He does care.
So change your view and trust in him
be a fool to God instead of men.
Believe in Him
follow by faith the footprints
matching His life plans with you.

Cassie and Cathy

Two sisters lived in a home
running a bed and breakfast business together
in the neck of the woods
a long drive away from the local neighbourhood.
Cassie greeted the guests
cooking the breakfast while helping clean the rooms
scurrying back and forth with the housekeeper.
Soon she soon spotted Cathy her sister
visiting with their unusual guest
while she was creating blisters.
Cassie saw while grinding her teeth
Cathy smiling and beckoning Cassie aside
as if there was time to set aside.
Rolling her eyes Cassie bit her tongue for once
one more breakfast to do she exhaled loudly
But this time she looked past the guests
gazing at the bearded man
she knew he saw through her tasks and plans.
Calling out to her staff to finish the meal
Cassie saw Cathy beaming at her
patting the seat beside her just in front of Him.
"Cassie, Cassie," smiled the man
"You worry too much about your plans

Cathy has been taking in what she needs
learning what is important
like the living water to a growing seed.
Glancing at her beaming sister
Cassie knelt before this man
willing to learn whispering to Him
Please continue to teach as I have much to learn.
"Blessed are you Cassie
leave your burden behind," He replied.
Gazing at His compassionate eyes
Cassie felt a heart filled with peace and grace
hugging her sister Cathy in genuine love.
just at that moment a sun beam approved
its morning warmth shared upon the three of them.

I Thank You Lord

I thank you Lord for my sight
gazing upon many marvelous views
while feeling the precious wind bending the trees
as the leaves fall onto their knees.
I thank you Lord
for my job, home, family too
maybe not yet a wife to woo.
It is time to be grateful
to the customers, bosses and co-workers
I thank you Lord for my health
it is truly the greatest gift of wealth.
Freedom to go where you please
Worshiping the Son without the police
a blessing that we take for granted every day.
I thank you Lord for the Son
our sins are forgiven and done
if we surrender then we have won.
Eternal praise to the heavens we seek
forget this temporary world that is so weak.
I thank you Lord
for the heartbeat of faith so abundant and in store.

For those who reach out to Him
will never be bored to the core.
Today I give thanks to you Lord.

The Gardening Vine

The gardener sets up the divine trellis
as he plants the eternal vine.
Some branches grow up sprouting towards the sun
as a few shrivel up in the weeds
while shadow seeds wither in the heat of our star.
Different events trigger differing reactions
a flourishing vine may wither
yet a weaker branch turns
growing strongly without a dither.
The gardener observes while sighing inward
as he sharply prunes many shriveled branches
then tossing them into the fire.
He begins watering the rest of the vine
the branches begin to choose one way or the other
for the gardener each branch has its own sign.
No branch trying to go alone
will escape the dire but necessary pruning.
For each branch the gardener has a special design
if the branch responds to the trim
more fruit will be grown filled to the brim.
No branch is a vine alone
so if the branch blossoms in the vine
the gardener blesses the vine

growing and stretching out that branch.
A branch asking for the vine to grow as it wishes
will be granted permission to carry on
remaining as a firm portion of the entire creation
enriching the vine to satisfy the branch and vine alike.
Slowly the entire plant is revealed to all
many branches exist as dry and brittle fit for the fire
as a large number integrate to the plan of the vine.
More blooms and fruit will be produced
attracting many others to be a divine branch
fulfilling the great commission of the great vine.
If you didn't guess or suspect
the gardener is the vine – the boss and the chief prospect.
Let this be a tale for the branches
stick closely and grow for the vine
the gardener's fertilizer and water will bless
eternal growth.
Go out on a limb on one's own choosing
The dried up branch will be cursed for eternal losing.
The vine desires each branch to blossom and win
not desiring the branch of yours to wither away in sin.
The vine and the gardener are together as one
each branch should intertwine in an obedient tone
the more fruit produced by these branches
the gardener's glory enhances
as the entire vine will be of an eternal worship
without death, without curses
the grand vine will be forever growing by the divine
design.

The Demons, the Hogs and the Cows

In a rural town lived this wild, unruly boy
all of his toys smashed while hissing and cursing.
In school he couldn't be trained
even with medication the boy was barely restrained.
School was an impossible dream
his parents and sister feared
his eye of unholy gleam.
In an evening paper was a coming revival
as the father pointed this out
the boy quaked in denial.
As the evening approached
the family got him into the car
then while driving down the country road
screeching from the possessed boy
scared even the passing frogs and toads.
Being late for the service
the parents dragged their son to the revival tent
guttural screams and foaming at the mouth
scaring many in the crowd.
But the preacher stopped his sermon
walking to the boy boldly and not cowed.
Don't cast us out – don't send us to the darkness
screeched the boy in an eerie evil tone.

Who are you demanded the preacher
looking at the boy in earnest.
Legion, we are many and don't wish to leave
the demons answered upfront to the preacher man.
You are not staying with the boy and no harm
will come to this child replied the man.
When I cast you out go back where you came from.
There's a herd of hogs and cows they pleaded
let us go into them.
The preacher obliged calling out
in the name of Jesus I command thee
to leave this boy immediately
leave and enter the hogs and the cows.
Now the boy writhed and fell to the ground
as the entire crowd stared intently and astounded
as the boy collapsed lying in peace.
Then an unholy lowing and squealing began
from the next field a hundred pigs and forty cows
fled down the hill into the river and drowned.
The boy stood up looking weak
asking his parents for something to eat.
The preacher stood beside the boy to say
here is a Bible
food for the soul you so desperately need.
Preacher man the boy replied
what can I do to serve who has saved me?
The parents and the preacher smiled
with a nod the minister replied.
I know you've had a hard ordeal
however go tell others

what Jesus did for you tonight
delivering you from evil bondage
in this night of the demons, the hogs and the cows
repentance brings the gift of Calvary to you.
The boy and his family prayed and repented
although the following day
some of the neighbours raised a fuss
how the preacher queerly somehow and in some way
sent their hogs and cows to a watery grave.
The police arrived along with the legal guns
finally the preacher was forced
to cancel his sermons and move on.
As he was leaving town he visited the little boy
who was shy but did not act coy
saying to him and his family
let him preach about his deliverance
show how gracious our Lord is from this day forward
for this town will never be the same again.

The Lost Stamp

An older lady had a hobby in collecting stamps
every topic and country in her collection was revamped.
Extensively recorded and added to an album
there was one stamp more valuable than all.
It was an 1840's British stamp
so rare that at an auction would have created
for somebody a small fortune.
A sentimental gift at heart passed down from
her great-grandfather
one morning while she opened up her stamp book
there was an opening as her favourite stamp was missing.
Alarmed she scurried across her home
searching everywhere from the couch to the coffee table
to the living room and the small desk
nowhere could this lady find her precious lost stamp.
Soon every friend or neighbour knew about the stamp
today the silver haired lady did not share a coffee
for she missed that lost stamp.
Shuffling into the kitchen
she examined the living room entrance again
spending the morning fretting to herself
checking her bed room and bathroom too.
The lady did not even eat her dinner

forgotten in her search the time that was spent
on her hands and knees a position uncomfortable
and bent.
Spotting this time a crack between the small desk and
the wall
she gazed upon a pencil while answering more
phone calls.
the lady explained her absence from the morning coffee
after the calls were made
she edged the desk away and spotted the kitten's
sponge ball
but then she spotted a square looking like...
She reached down and picked up what appeared to be
a stamp
while turning over it was the lost 1840's English stamp.
The lost stamp had been found!
Smiling she danced on the floor and picked up the phone
inviting friends and neighbours over for a coffee.
In an hour she had a large gathering
to learn the news of the fruits of her labour.
"My friends," the lady squealed
what was given up for lost has now been found.
My precious stamp fell behind the desk on the rebound.
Celebrate with me today
have some coffee and cookies in a merry way.
What was lost now is found
the value of which is priceless beyond compare.
The gathering erupted in cheers and applause
as she placed the stamp in a new glass display case
lost but now found

the old lady now secured the stamp for as long as she
lived.

The Swimming Pool

In a small dusty rural town
the local swimming pool was open
on a beautiful hot sunny day
the heat of the sun beams down
the only relief came from a quantity of cool water
as a drought had hit this town some time ago.
There was a young, brown haired man sitting in
a wheelchair
drinking a nip of whisky furtively from his flask
looking on wistfully
as the crowd of people entered and left the pool.
An ordinary older man with a hint of grey in his beard
wearing shabby blue clothes with sunglasses
walked up to the young man asking how he was doing.
"My arthritis and multiple sclerosis is so bad
I can barely walk yet now wish
I could wade in the pool to bring relief without pain."
The grey bearded man lowered his sunglasses
and answered
"Do you really want to be well?"
"I have no one to help me get in or out of the pool,"
the younger man complained in reply.
The grey bearded man gazed seriously

at the young man then commanded
"Pick up your chair and walk into the water."
Instantly the crippled man stood up
carrying his chair he then realized that he had no pain
feeling like a brand new man.
Turning around the grey bearded man had disappeared
so the young man walked with confidence
into the deep end of the pool he waded.
The lifeguard blew his whistle
a doctor came up from his chair
to talk to the walking young man.
"How did you walk into here?" the lifeguard demanded
as the doctor nodded in agreement.
The grey bearded man in blue clothes did this
answered the walking man in reply.
He wore sunglasses and had the skin
of a Middle East tan.
The doctor interrupted at that point
see here I know you have been crippled for a long time
how can this possibly be?
The grey bearded man asked if I wanted to get well.
Then I told him I couldn't go into the water
but the older man said to pick up your chair
get up and go enter the water.
Befuddled the lifeguard and doctor
stopped asking questions
as the man stepped out of the water.
Entering the parking lot he got his car to drive home
as a police car with sirens blaring arrived on the scene.
Out of the car arrive the same grey bearded man

wearing sunglasses and his police uniform.
Walking over to the young man's car he said,
"I'm giving you a warning ticket this time son.
You are well again now
so stop the drinking and the consequent sinning
or you will suffer a fate worse than death.
Go tell the lifeguard and doctor my answer."
With that the police officer smiled
as he entered his own car and drove away.
The young man went back to the pool
telling the lifeguard and the doctor what had happened.
They were baffled and not quite believed
as the young man went back to his car.
He took out his flask
emptying out the booze on the side of the street
then tossed the flask into a garbage can
his thoughts wandered as he drove home
pondering the day he had spent at the swimming pool.

The Catcher of the Fishes

The fisherman casts day and night
by sunlight or moonlight his boat floats far and wide
a wide swath of the sea he does abide.
Sometimes heavy sometimes light
always he brings a fresh harvest of fish
to the sorting area for the men on the docks.
The men on the docks begin their work
some fish are rotten they are tossed aboard
to be devoured by the dark creatures of the deep.
Others appear to be fresh and alive
two fish are filleted up side by side
the inside of one is fresh and clean
the other rotten inside and put aside
as Fisherman's helpers they separate
the good fish from the bad.
The rotten fish are tossed into the deep waters
to be devoured below once and for all.
The fish which are fresh and good
no matter how few

handed over to the fisherman by the crew.
He takes them up to the house of the owner
set aside for dining with the master.

Tossed into a fresh aquarium
the fish return alive to their surprise.
One day the good fish will dive into an eternal
blessed ocean
for the rotten fish there will be a silent commotion
lost for all time in a pitch black abyss
cast away from the aquamarine paradise.

The fisherman heads out every day
one day every fish will be caught
whether good on the inside
for the fish it is for naught
then if it is internally rotten
a terrible lesson will be taught.
The catcher of the fishes
does not account for mere wishes.
The standard for selecting the good fish from the bad
everyone knows how this will go
so how will things turn out
each individual fish
must make a choice one way or the next.

Take This Away

Write down a few words this I will do
the thoughts stuck together just like glue
what to write I don't have a clue.
Each word like life is on a different path
some are cherry blossoms
while others exist as a life of wrath.
Is it well in my soul
does it feel like a lump of heavy coal?
Take this away Jesus
I fail you every day
drifting alone I do not hold sway.
As a flock of geese fly by in the blue sky
while pondering God's marvelous creations
I feel like broken pottery made out of clay.
Let us not be controlled by emotions
Trust in God when you need to lean hard
go to the source of love and protection – the
master Bard.
Do not fold
hold on to play the last card
do not be swayed by the waves of emotion
but stand firm as the Rock of salvation.
as you put your faith in Jesus

love Him with all and everything
He will not hold back anything.
Praise you Jesus, thank you God
when the clouds obscure a setting sun
even then the light pierces through before the star
does set.

Faith By an Indian Woman

A doctor walked on the sandy beach
as the evening sun began sinking into the western sky.
Some of his friends and neighbours
joined him while walking back to town
after opening up a free medical clinic for that day.
An Indian woman walked behind the group
shouting out clearly to the sky
"Doctor, my son is possessed by the devil.
"Healer help me please heal him."
She repeated this cry several times
as several of the doctor's friends glared at her
but she called out fervently and persistently.
One man said to the doctor
"Let us send her away
the day is nearly over for us."
Stopping in his tracks
the doctor shook his head vehemently in reply.
"My duty is to tend to the lost sheep
no matter the time of the day."
The woman walked up in front of the doctor
kneeling before him she pled, "Healer, help me."
Looking at the Indian woman with compassion
he replied

"It is not proper to take a child's food
and toss on it on the floor for the cat."
But the woman confidently replied,
"Yes it is proper Healer. Even the cats eat
the crumbs off the master's table."
The healer smiled widely as he answered
"Blessed are you, woman of great faith.
Your request for you son's deliverance has been granted."
The lady smiled and hugged the healer
as the crowd gazed in amazement.
She left to go home for it was an hour's walk
her son and the entire family met her half way back
as he told her when he was healed.
She smiled with grace
Telling her story to the amazed family what
had occurred.
It was the exact moment
when the doctor had granted her wish
that her son was cured of the affliction.
The family celebrated on the woman's behalf
that the doctor had granted her desires
by faith her son had been healed.

Hang into the Wind

Wind gusts slam into you
tossed around like a tornado ball.
What can you do then?
Hang into the wind
hold on tight
as the gale force brings itself to the full height.
Don't let there be a heist
allowing your dreams, skills and abilities to fly away.
Let it be cold
hang into the wind.
do not be blown away
allowing your soul to grow mould.
Do not be led astray
every Rock holds steady in its place.
Be still and appreciate now
with the divine forces hammering on your bow
getting your full attention.
Hang into the wind
let Jesus take you where you both want to go.
Your desires and His purposes
one and the same.
Hang into the wind
it is time to take a stand and grow.

The Old Pensioner

An elderly grey haired pensioner looked up at the steps
he glanced towards the cross while racked with pain
sitting outside the entranceway of the busy church.
The cross shone like the colour of harvest gold
while it was roped off
with a sign to deter vandals
saying in bold letters "Do not touch!"
The old pensioner had lived a decent life
his wife having passed away a few years ago
their only child tragically disappearing
never to be seen again.
Being diagnosed with advanced cancer
his dwindling funds paying for treatments
the golden cross beckoned to him.
For some reason the old pensioner
never considered the meaning of the cross at Calvary.
Today many people sauntered into the church.
As the crowd drew around him to go inside
the old man touched the golden cross passing by
thinking that it may help him for a cure.
Instantly his strength returned
as a powerful warmth flowed through him
somehow he knew something miraculous had occurred.

A siren buzzed on top of the cross
as the crowd froze and turned around
as the pastor rushed out shouting
"Who touched the cross?"
The crowd milled about
not knowing what the old pensioner did.
After the pastor again shouted the same question
the old man stepped in front of the clergyman.
"Pastor, I have cancer
with constant pain and no resources.
I was attracted to the cross thinking I could be cured
so as I touched it a powerful warmth has come over me
and my strength has returned."
The pastor's face glowed as he cried out
"Bless you sir," proclaimed the pastor.
"It is not the cross but He who is on the cross
dying for your sins.
Yes He is the one who healed you."
"Your faith has made you well sir.
Come in to our church
we will celebrate in our service
for today another lost sheep has come home."

Seed of Growth

As soon as man begins to grow
the changes come in a steady flow.
Man has no control over the growth
like a seed planted in the ground.
Soon this seed sprouts and grows in spurts
mankind cannot start this kind of bloom.

The heart of man
seeded and watered by God
flourishes in the good soil
that man does not comprehend.
The soil grows the plant
the stalk, the head and the full kernel of grain
maturing in the knowledge of God.
When the grain is ripe and the heart is ready
a divine sickle swings down steady
the harvest of the soul arrives on schedule.
The seed of growth passes through another cycle
a bounty enriched by a heavenly designed divine plan.

The Farmer Next in Line

The farmer sat down on a lumpy bench
in the old brown coffee shop
right on main street for serious gossip and talk.
His friends gathered around young and old
for the gray haired man raised his dusty farmer's cap.
"I've finally retired now," he announced.
"I handed over the operation over to my son."
"Which one?" a bearded friend asked.
"Let me tell you how it happened,"
the farmer replied.
I have two sons as you know
for the one goal to owning my operation.
So I set them both a task to complete within a single day
although I knew neither one would be finished that day.
Michael, my oldest, is a design engineer
but not cut out for mechanical stuff
as I asked him to swatch the canola field.
"Sorry, Dad," he said, "I've got a project
for my firm that needs to be finished."
So I called Oliver, his youngest brother.
You know the one keen on farming as my right
hand man.
"Okay Dad I'll start right after dinner," Oliver replied

walking out to go service the tractors
as Michael held his tablet steady
creating architectural drawings that make my head spin.
The farmer stopped for a sip of coffee
I told the boys I'm heading off to Blakeshaw
an hour drive away to get some parts
and fill up some shopping carts with toys.
There were two tractors ready to swath the canola
I gave them my final instructions to them then
and there.
I traveled to Blakeshaw without a care
my trip went quicker than expected
so I drove into the yard without warning.
One tractor was in the yard the other one in the field.
There was Oliver sitting on the porch playing cards with
his friends.
Glancing at his bearded friend, the farmer continued
his tale.
I chewed Oliver out up and down the steps
soon the other tractor roared up to the shop.
To my surprise Michael broke a sweat
as there were tears in his eyes.
I ran over to the shop as he began to fix something.
"Michael what's the matter?" I shouted.
A belt broke and he needed to fix it Michael replied.
My engineering project was canceled and I lost my job.
My head was spinning so I went out swathing canola
knowing that the job had to be done.
So I went out to swath to clear my head and think of
what to do next.

I told Michael that I was proud of him today.
Then the farmer gazed at the coffee crowd
hushed by the ending of the story.
"Two sons, one goal,
which one of the sons did I give the farm too?"
"Would it be the son who said no but came back and did
the work anyhow
or to the son who agreed to work but never showed up?"
The bearded friend said, "Michael,"
"That's right friend," nodded the farmer.
It's not what one says
but the actions that prove
the character of man.
He who does the father's work
will inherit the business
to be the next farmer in line.

Ginsweth the Broker

A sharply dressed investor broker named Ginsweth
looked for the arriving teacher to make his sermon.
A large crowd taller than he prevented him to see
the man
by a well known evangelist known all around
for Ginsweth was intrigued but not cowed.
A questionable character in his own business
Ginsweth was shunned by local society.
The short, dark-haired man set up a step ladder
standing above the crowd to view the preacher
a fiery red-haired man without the temperament
to match.
As the evangelist drew near
he looked up and announced
"Ginsweth, come down I want to have supper with you."
Ginsweth came down the ladder as the
crowd murmured
about the evangelist dealing with this crooked man.
"Teacher," replied Ginsweth, "come to my home."
"But first if I have overcharged anyone I shall
pay them back plus double of what I took.
Then if I have cheated many, I will pay each of these
people five times what I took."

The evangelist smiled as he shook Ginsweth's hand.
"Ginsweth let us take supper now.
For tonight salvation will come to the house
of Ginsweth the broker."

Raymond and the Businessman

There lived in the city a rich businessman
prosperous with plenty of profit in the kitty.
He and his brothers owned a chain of stores.
One long time employee Raymond
worked hard as a loyal staff member.
The rich businessman scoffed at his efforts
refusing to give him a raise.
Raymond went to another business to find work
praying for the rich businessman
who mocked him and acted like a jerk.
The rich businessman threatened the other man
to let Raymond go and smiled when he got his wish.
Raymond struggled on welfare to fill his food dish.
Soon Raymond lost his home when he missed
his payments
as the rich businessman bought more homes
partying like there was no tomorrow.

On the same day both men died
Raymond on the streets from exposure
while the rich businessman attended a fancy party
had a heart attack and then died.

Instantly both men ended up in different
eternal directions.
The rich businessman suffered in the agonies of hell
while Raymond lived peacefully in paradise.
One day an angel brought Raymond
to the border of the black abyss.
The rich businessman and Raymond stared at
one another
the tormented man cried out,
"Please angel, give me a bottle cap full of water
to sooth my burning tongue."
The angel shook his head but replied,
"You sir had all the finer things in life.
Raymond worked hard and was loyal
but you treated him badly
while Raymond lived a godly life and now has
his reward.
Besides which there is no possible way
to cross this divide between heaven and hell.
The rich businessman begged him once more,
"Fair enough I've earned my lot
but please warn my brothers.
Go send them a preacher to share the news
to keep them from the fate of mine."
The angel replied with a sigh,
"God has appointed pastors to your town
in which your family has mocked and frowned upon.
Let your brothers hear the message
and be saved from the ministers appointed there.
We will never pass this way again.

Indeed let the rich businessman
ponder his eternal fate that he has chosen."
Raymond spoke to the businessman
to the surprise of all of them.
"Farewell sir. You didn't listen to the message
but now it is too late for you."
The rich businessman sobbed
as Raymond and the angel departed forevermore.

Lionel and the Tramp Lady

A young man named Lionel
walked through the dark streets of a bad neighbourhood
searching for his sister in the dark echoes of the ghetto.
A gang of thugs pounced on him
beating and stabbing the man nearly to death.
He groaned on the street with his broken glasses on
the ground
the wallet and watch merely stolen.
First the mayor drove up to him in a luxury car
he told Lionel, "Don't worry I'll be back with help, not
too fear."
Getting back into his limousine he drove away.
A few minutes later a local pastor
cautiously walked up to the man,
nervous about the dangerous neighbourhood
he blessed Lionel yet scurried away.
Lying in despair the young man pondered about
his death
when a tramp lady staggered up to him.
Having been drinking she heard Lionel whisper,
"Find my sister I failed to aid her."
The tramp lady took a look at her drugs and booze
then sold them to another dealer.

She called a cab
riding alongside Lionel to the hospital.
He was placed into emergency surgery
as the tramp lady held out a thick wad of bills
donating what money she had
paying for the urgent medical care
before quickly exiting the hospital.
Several days later
the homeless tramp startled Lionel by visiting him.
"Thea? Is that you sister?" he exclaimed.
"Yes brother I've come to take you to my shelter,
you need to recover," Thea replied with a sad smile.
Getting dressed together the two of them
walked down towards the exit.
Spotting the mayor and pastor waiting for an elevator
Lionel nodded to his sister
speaking to both of the men,
"Do you recognize my sister Mr. Mayor or pastor?"
Both men were shocked
at Thea's ragged and skinny appearance.
Lionel continued speaking
while putting on his glasses.
"Do you not remember me?
A few days ago I was beaten up and left for dead
going to help my sister in need
to ask forgiveness for neglecting her.
You mayor drove on by and forgot
that the ghetto is part of your city.
Pastor you neglected your flock
too, afraid to reach out.

This tramp lady here came and rescued me
a sibling whether biological or not, it does not matter.
Lionel hugged the surprised lady then said
"You are my sister and I am your brother."
Speaking to the stunned trio
"Which of the three of you did the Lord's work
who was the one that helped
when I needed dire assistance?
It was Thea the modern day homeless one
who showed love and concern."
Two of the three bowed their heads
in shame as recognition set in for the pair of them.
"Do you recognize me now?" Lionel asked
I was elected premier of this province recently
now my sister Thea will have her life restored.
Please help the others, a teary eyed
Thea whispered to her brother.
Yes we will go down to see what needs to be done to help
but you are staying with me to restore your life.
As for you mayor and pastor
beware that this won't happen to you
without anyone coming to your rescue.
Lionel and the tramp lady left to a waiting limo to
his home
as the other two watched in an awkward silence.

Our Song

In the name of Christ
today our lives belong to him
our lives, our testimony, our song
either the sounds of discordant screeching
or the verses of singing in harmony.

For better or for worse
do we live with the Lord verse by verse?
His grace abounds
his love a bottomless sea
the currents of faith flow
from the common housefly
to the far end of the cosmos.

How did God create the cosmos?
While gazing at the constellations
couple the vastness together
with the immense complexity of the universe.
Can we understand the question
how or why God did this?
Examine the depths of the ocean
the secrets of the deep blue sea still undiscovered.
Can we understand his majesty

while climbing mountain tops or hiking on trails.
Venture into the bush
observe a bear, a moose or a deer.
Altogether God speaks or sings to us
in an endless variety of ways.
Jesus the Son, Jesus is Lord
God's song is a precious gift.
With God's perfect harmony and pitch
our song together shows grace to a world
desperate in need without the heart of knowledge.
Let the peace of Him
bring dreams and hopes alive today.

Love, Hope and Faith

Live a love life
love is life
love means living
sacrifice without asking but by giving
Hope from the promise of the future
on faith we must choose to nurture
In the name of our God
give praise to Him
through trials and tribulation.
Faith will grow like a mustard tree
the smallest seed growing to a looming giant of a tree.
Thank you Jesus for your love
Thank you God for our family
Bless the sick and the lonely
shower love onto the widows and the homely
I know you are there God
not just with the thoughts in my brain
It is time to clean my head and my heart
to be more like you every day
Love, hope and faith are intertwined
love is the binding that holds life together combined

The Principle of Forgiveness

A scientist chatted away with his peers
a modest man with accolades galore
as the others viewed him as a mentor.
One of the group invited the scientist
over to his home for a meal.
The scientist agreed against his better thoughts
perhaps these fellows can be humbled and taught.
As the scientist entered the mansion house
he recognized a student who he had failed for cheating.
The student was now the butler
hanging up the scientist's coat first
as the others didn't give the butler a second glance.
Joseph invited them to the living room
as the owner and the host of this evening.
The butler arranged the best seat
saving the best wine for the scientist at his side.
After the drinks were served
the butler offered the finest food
Then the butler gave an expensive journal
to the preeminent scientist who nodded his thanks.
The butler shined his shoes next
as Joseph frowned his disbelief at the man's nerve
glaring and dismissing the butler out of the room.

The scientist read the owner's thoughts
thinking how to deliver a message to be taught.
"Joseph, I wish to tell you something," he said.
"Go ahead I am all ears," answered Joseph with pleasure.
"Joseph, two people owed money to a local bank.
One man owed five thousand dollars
the other man five hundred dollars.
Neither man could pay the bank back.
so the banker decided
to forgive both of them all of their debt.
Tell me Joseph who will be the more grateful?
"The man who owed five thousand," Joseph said.
Correct. Do you see your butler?
He took off my coat and shined my shoes.
He gave me an expensive journal that he could afford
as well as offering the finest seat and wine
You on the other hand offered me nothing.
Yet I know about
the cheating scandal at the school years ago.
You and the butler both were guilty
but he humbled himself first tonight.
Joseph you have forgotten
the principle of forgiveness.
Joseph frowned as the butler came back in.
Looking at the butler's gaze the scientist commented
The principle of forgiveness says this:
He is who is forgiven much will love much
but he who is forgiven little will love little.
Young man quit your butler job
I have a place of integrity for a man like you.

Joseph and the other guest frowned and murmured
as the butler stepped forward to remove his uniform
The scientist interrupted his reply,
"Young man your repentance has saved you.
Meet me at the university headquarters
at half past eight tomorrow morning."
With peace and contentment in his heart
the scientist walked into the dining room to eat.

The Other Daughter

There once lived a family with the parents
three daughters, including a set of twins.
The twins Jeanne and Davita
worked at their parents clothing store
as a successful upmarket business in a mega city.
Liz the youngest daughter became dissatisfied
always known as the other daughter.
One day Liz announced she was moving out on her own
taking her share of the inheritance as a loan.
The twins were both disgusted
while the parents shook their heads like a windy gust
as Liz walked out with her phone and used car.
She started a part time job at a bar
but soon Liz got hooked on booze and drugs.
She stole money to pay off the dealer thugs
she lost a lot of weight snorting up cocaine.
One day Liz woke up, her job barely keeping her alive
remembering the life she had behind
before wasting her inheritance in the store.

Liz staggered out of her apartment
as she walked up to her family's house.
Remorse came to the center of her heart
as her mother opened up the front door to a
Christmas return.
Liz begged her mother to forgive her
she plead for mercy on her knees.
"Come up on your feet Liz," shouted the joyous father.

He sent for the twins
Come quick your other sister Elizabeth has returned.
The mother made plans for a returning party
to create a large meal tasty and hearty.
Yet the twins frowned at Liz
as she could not find words to say to them.
"What's the matter with you
Jeanne and Davita?" their mother asked.
They answered, "We never get a family party.
Look, we have worked hard for you
nor have we wasted an inheritance.
Just look at how awful Liz looks."
"Do not complain," scolded the father.
"One day you may wander astray
needing to come home for a stay.
Your sister who we have misjudged
as the other daughter
she was lost but now is found
Liz has repented and is forgiven."
The twins paused then ran towards
Liz the other sister and hugged her.

As the three of them sobbed together
first in sadness then in joy.
The proud parents clapped
as the father exalted the family.
"That's my girls.
Today this party will be
a celebration for all of them."

Overseer

Depression is stuck in my heart
the self-hatred in my thoughts
plague my mind galore
as a quiet despair occupies my heart
how do i understand?
In dealing with the inner war
while fending off the armed black angel
attacking with his emotional sword
the cold blade cutting with the black coal of hell
Self-destructive images
the ongoing battle rages in the soul
constant negativity runs amok
a lifeline is needed now
Where is a psalm to calm the soul?
Lord Jesus I'm pressed to the max
my faith is weak and lax
Uplift my thoughts out of the muck
your LOVE is greater than any bad luck
Thank you God for your love

at Calvary you showed how much you care
I appeal to you my King
forgive me for forsaking you
show me a clean heart
to obey and never forget you Jesus
my soul is bone dry today
seeking to be soaked in your rain clouds of love
Send a flood to overflow the banks of my soul
All the glory and thanks go to you
Praise you Jesus
shepherd of the universe
caring for me if I was the only one
let the love flow through me with abound
turn my heart around
release the hate
deflate the fear
let my heart be free and be unwound
Praise be to God
author of the universe
victor above all stress and strife
Glory for Jesus you are my lord
I praise you that today I shall be restored
by faith in your name
We ask We believe
your will be done
on earth to fulfill heaven's will
Thank you Jesus for your victory
over sin known as death
Be my overseer God
in my failings

you pursue and follow with no relent
my own efforts are hollow
Praise to you Jesus
let your joy refill my soul
Hallowed be your name
these are three "yous" for the king and overseer
Thank you, praise you, love and obey you
Your name is everything
without you I am nothing
Praise you Jesus
thank you El-Shaddai
Shepherd to every child of yours
be my overseer take over my heart
anything good be added to your name
remove the sin remove the depression
throw it so far away
in every direction
you cannot ever find it again
Amen!

The Party

A wealthy business leader wished to stage
for his only son
a grand twenty-first birthday.
He phoned, emailed, and tweeted galore
to esteemed colleagues, friends and associates
to his surprise and shock no one replied
except for a few sneers of contempt.
The man postponed the event for a day
reassuring his son that his birthday would be a
grand event.
He sent several of his aides to invite them personally
but the aides were robbed, their cars vandalized
as they returned beaten the wealthy leader
was scandalized.
Sending in lawyers and thugs
he burned down their homes
arresting and suing the rest
utterly ruining them in every possible way.
Furious the man demanded that his staff
invite anyone and everyone off the street
even if they were criminals with intent.
The staff followed the instructions to the letter
as his home filled up the man felt better.

Every guest had a bar code scanned on a name badge
while the people had a great time.
Except for that one of the original invitees snuck into
the house
the son told the enraged father
who gathered the man by the arm
"Where is your badge as you are not on the guest list?"
demanded the angry leader.
The guest stood silent and dumb founded
as the wealthy father called security
instructing him to throw him out
handcuffing the intruder to the tree outside
so he could hear the party and celebration
yet gnash his teeth in frustration.
The man turned to his son
watching the security remove the unwanted guest
to the son he spoke an eloquent line
that many will remember to the end of their time.
"So many are invited to the main event
but only a precious few will be chosen to attend."

The Crops in the Field

As the seeding season began
the farmer went out into his fields
with his tractor and seed drill
his hired hands helped plant canola
in search of a bountiful yield.
Yet a jealous neighbour knew
the crop had the potential to fill all the granaries
in a harvest bountiful and plentiful.
The jealous man snuck out one night
planting thistles where it was empty.
The rains fell at their appointed time
in no time at all the crops grew up tall.
The hired men noticed many thistle patches
then went to the farmer and asked
"Boss you planted good canola seed
we know this, yet for this crop in the field
there are thistle weeds in too many patches."
"A jealous neighbour did this," answered the farmer.
"Should get go pull up the weeds by hand?"
"No because you may uproot the good canola plants."
The farmer continued on with his instructions.
Let this crop bloom into a solid field of yellow blooms
then we shall take out and spray the crops in this field

sweeping the weeds clean
like a broom removing the dust from the kitchen floor.
Then we will harvest the bounty
the granaries filled up with the bounty.
Whatever shriveled up left overs remain
we spray again and only in this field do we burn
the stubble.
As for the jealous neighbour
I will soon give him the gears
for no longer will he cause trouble anymore
to any crops in the field.

Worry Ends Where?

As the rising bustle of the retail Christmas draws near
acquisition of materialism increases day by day.
Attempts to find the perfect gift
while driving to and fro prove to be fruitless.
Even many people who believe
get caught up rat race trap to deceive
for as the phrase goes
worry ends where faith begins.
Pondering this thought after taking a photo
the Christmas tree stood by
with the nativity scene on the table next beside it.
The sign perched behind the scene states
worry ends where?
The perfect free gift at Calvary
begins at the nativity scene at the manger.
Our Saviour died as the ultimate sacrifice
salvation coming at the highest cost
our selfish desires to be crucified nailed to the cross.
Slow down and love your neighbour
listen to a friend help a family member
pray for peace, the lonely and the sick.
Family is where the manger begins.
Mary and Joesph and the shepherds

the angels guiding the three kings by the star.
Biblical prophecies all coming true tonight.
The crux of human history coming to a fruitful climax.
Remember the scene at the manger
when the phrase comes to mind
worry ends where?

The Shepherds

It was the usual quiet night
Dave, Nate and myself were together
on a bright moonlit night herding the sheep.
Calm and quiet it was with the grazing sheep
but suddenly a blinding light appeared
an angel towered over us in the sky.
My legs trembled as I felt my face turn white
no doubt the same as Dave and Nate felt.
The angel smiled at us and said,
"Do not be afraid
I bring good news and great joy for all people.
Today in the town of David
a Saviour, called the Messiah, he has been born.
The sign to you is a baby born
wrapped in cloths lying in a manger."
After this startling announcement
a huge company of heavenly hosts sang
Glory to God in the highest heaven
and peace on Earth to those whom his favour rests on.
After the angels left I said to Dave and Nate,
"Let us hurry to Bethlehem boys and see the Saviour."
We all agreed and hurried down the road
headed towards Bethlehem following the star

after a short while we found the manger.
Following Nate and Dave
we greeted Joseph and Mary and then gazed upon
the child.
Those beautiful eyes I always remember
a babe yet with divine knowledge and love in those eyes.
Nate nudged me as I was startled and lost in thought
"We must share the news with Bethlehem
that our Saviour was born and lives among us."
I told Joesph and Mary
what the angels spoke and how we came to be here.
All were amazed while Mary quietly thought
about what we had told her.
So the three of us went into town
shouting and calling out to all we met.
The Saviour is born. Our Messiah has returned.
I don't remember how many times
repeating the wondrous news was a wonderful chime.
Everyone was amazed and marveled at the news
but soon the three of us returned to the manger.
The name "Immanuel" came to my heart
as we rushed back to the manger.
Praise God, Glory to him
for Immanuel our King has been born.
The salvation of Israel has arrived I noted
blessed are those who believe on sight
but a greater blessing to those
believing without seeing this
miracle by God tonight.
Prophets and kings wished to see this

yet we mere shepherds
were guided here by the angels of the most High.
Everyone gazed at me wide eyed
as Dave and Nate gawked at me.
Three wise men nodded and smiled at me.
Joseph and Mary smiled
as we all praised God.
Soon we took leave of the newborn King.
Going back home to the fields Nate said to me,
"Why did you say that?
You sounded like a prophet."
I am a shepherd but Immanuel spoke to my heart
I complied with no choice but to state the message.
My friends nodded in understanding.
In this story known as the shepherds
our names do not matter.
We will tell everyone
therefore we will live for the true King.
Tonight was the birth of God's son.
I nodded as we walked back to our field of sheep
knowing what we would be dreaming about
this very night and in the nights to come.

Author's Bio

Quinn Graw has been writing poetry since 1992. He enjoys writing on a variety of subjects and has published two poetry books, The Spring Rain and Time Cube: Echoes of Life's Highway. Quinn enjoys reading, playing cards, as well as following hockey and Canadian football. He currently resides and works in his hometown of Manning, Alberta.

CPSIA information can be obtained at www.ICGtesting.com
Printed in the USA
LVOW11s0405070716

495231LV00006B/110/P